To Linda and John, for being
such nice neighbors
– CF

For Mik, with love
– GH

tiger tales
an imprint of ME Media, LLC
202 Old Ridgefield Road, Wilton, CT 06897
Published in the United States 2004
Originally published in Great Britain 2004 by Little Tiger Press
An imprint of Magi Publications
Text copyright © 2004 Claire Freedman
Illustrations copyright © 2004 Gaby Hansen
CIP data is available
ISBN 1-58925-037-0
Printed in Singapore
All rights reserved
1 3 5 7 9 10 8 6 4 2

Oops-a-Daisy!

by Claire Freedman
Illustrated by Gaby Hansen

tiger tales

There was a lot of jumping and thumping over in the meadow. Mama Rabbit was teaching Daisy how to hop.

"I'm going to try hopping all by myself!" Daisy cried excitedly. "Watch me, Mama!"

Daisy took a huge leap, lost her balance, and fell over backward!

"Never mind!" said Mama Rabbit.
"Try again."
So Daisy did...

hippity-hoppity flop!

hoppity-floppity whoops!

"I don't think I can do it, Mama!" Daisy cried.

"No one gets it right the first time," said Mama Rabbit, picking up Daisy and dusting her off. "Look at Little Mouse over by the duck pond."

Mama Mouse was showing Little Mouse
how to climb grass to reach the golden seeds
at the top.

Little Mouse inched closer and closer to the top. She had almost reached the seeds when . . .

slippity-flippity!

Little Mouse slid down again with a bump!
"Learning new things can be hard for
everyone!" Daisy said.

Daisy decided to practice little bunny hops.
"Stay in a straight line," Mama Rabbit called. "That's it!"
Up down, up down wobbled Daisy through
the tall grass.
"Hooray, I can do it!" she cried.
"Small hops are easier!"

Daisy saw a big molehill ahead.
She jumped a huge jump . . .

whoopsity-oopsity!

"Ouch! Who put that prickly thistle there?" Daisy said. "And why won't my feet do what I tell them to?"

"They will, in time!" said Mama.
She picked up Daisy and gave her
a hug. "Have you seen the mess
Little Badger is making?"

Little Badger was out in the field,
learning how to dig tunnels...

crashity-smashity!

Another one of his tunnels collapsed.
Little Badger and Daddy Badger were getting
muddier and muddier.

"I'm glad I'm not the only one who needs more practice,"
giggled Daisy.

Daisy and Mama Rabbit rested by the duck pond. Blue-green dragonflies darted around them whizzily-busily.

"Ribbit!" A big frog hopped out through the tall grass.

"I wish I could jump like that!" said Daisy. "Do you think I ever will?"

"You'll jump even higher!" Mama replied.

"Really?" cried Daisy, leaping up. "I'll try some more!"

"One, two . . . one, two," counted Daisy as she bounced. "Whee, look at me! Hopping is fun!"

"That's much better," Mama Rabbit called. "Oh no! Watch out, Daisy!" . . .

bumpity-thumpity!

Daisy slithered down the slippery
bank and skidded into the pond!
"Ribbit, ribbit!" croaked the frog
in surprise.
"Help!" Daisy cried. "I'm stuck
in the mud!"

Mama Rabbit ran down and pulled Daisy free.

"I was so busy counting that I didn't see the pond," sighed Daisy. "There's so much to remember all at once!"

"Cheer up, Daisy," Mama Rabbit said. "Let's practice together." Paw in paw, Daisy and Mama Rabbit hopped and skipped around the duck pond.

Little Duckling was out on the
water, practicing his swimming.
"Little Duckling isn't doing
very well," said Daisy. "He can
only swim in tiny circles!"
Then suddenly…

splashity-crashity!

Little Duckling sailed right into some water lilies! Quickly his mother swam across to untangle him.

"There's someone else who didn't look where they were going!" Mama Rabbit smiled.

Daisy laughed. "I'm going to try hopping by myself one more time!" she said.

Up down, up down bounced Daisy.
Wibbly-wobbly, hippity-hoppity hop!
   "That's it!" cried Mama. "Keep going!"
   "Did you see how high I jumped?" called Daisy proudly.
"I was almost flying! I can do it, Mama! I can do it!"
   "Well done, Daisy!" said Mama Rabbit. "You're hopping!"

Daisy hopped...

and skipped...

and jumped.

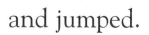

At last her legs were too
tired to keep hopping!
"I'll have to carry you home
this evening!" Mama laughed.

Happily, Daisy climbed into Mama Rabbit's arms and buried herself snuggly-huggly into her soft warm fur.

"Do you think Little Mouse, Little Badger, and Little Duckling learned how to climb and dig and swim?" Daisy asked Mama sleepily.

"I'm sure they did!" Mama
Rabbit whispered. "In the end!"